This book belongs to:

_____

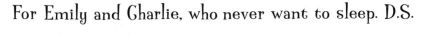

For Emily and Charlie, who never want to sleep. D.S.

For Baby Emily, may you be a good sleeper!
For Rose and Olivia, sweet dreams. H.S.

First published in Great Britain in 2012 by Andersen Press Ltd.,
20 Vauxhall Bridge Road, London SW1V 2SA.

Published in Australia by Random House Australia Pty.,
Level 3, 100 Pacific Highway, North Sydney, NSW 2060.

Colour separated in Switzerland by Photolitho AG, Zürich.
Printed and bound in Singapore by Tien Wah Press.

Holly Swain has used concentrated watercolour and colour pencil in this book.

10 9 8 7 6 5 4 3 2 1

British Library Cataloguing in Publication Data available.
ISBN 978 1 84939 006 4 (hardback) ISBN 978 1 84939 227 3 (paperback)
This book has been printed on acid-free paper

The King Who Wouldn't Sleep

Debbie Singleton   Holly Swain

Andersen Press

Many years ago, in a palace far across the sea, there lived a king, a queen and, of course, a beautiful princess.

The princess slept in a silver bed.

The queen slept in a golden bed.

And the king . . .

well, the king had no bed at all, because he never slept. Not a wink!

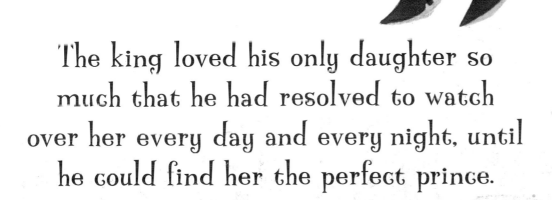

The king loved his only daughter so much that he had resolved to watch over her every day and every night, until he could find her the perfect prince.

Unfortunately it was not easy to find a perfect prince.

The king
met tall princes
and short princes,
strong princes and weak
princes, blond princes and
bald princes (and even one with
an extraordinary moustache).

But in the end he sent each one
away because not one of them
was quite perfect.

But did those princes give up and slink back to their castles?
No, they certainly did not. They realized that if they could just put the king to sleep, they would be able to talk to the princess.

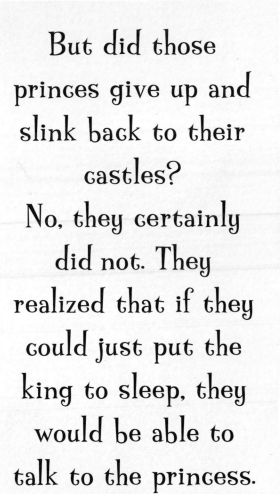

So they tried everything they could think
of to make the king fall asleep.

But the king wasn't so easily fooled.
He gave all the gifts to his servants . . .

... then got a bit cross when there was no one left awake to cook his dinner.

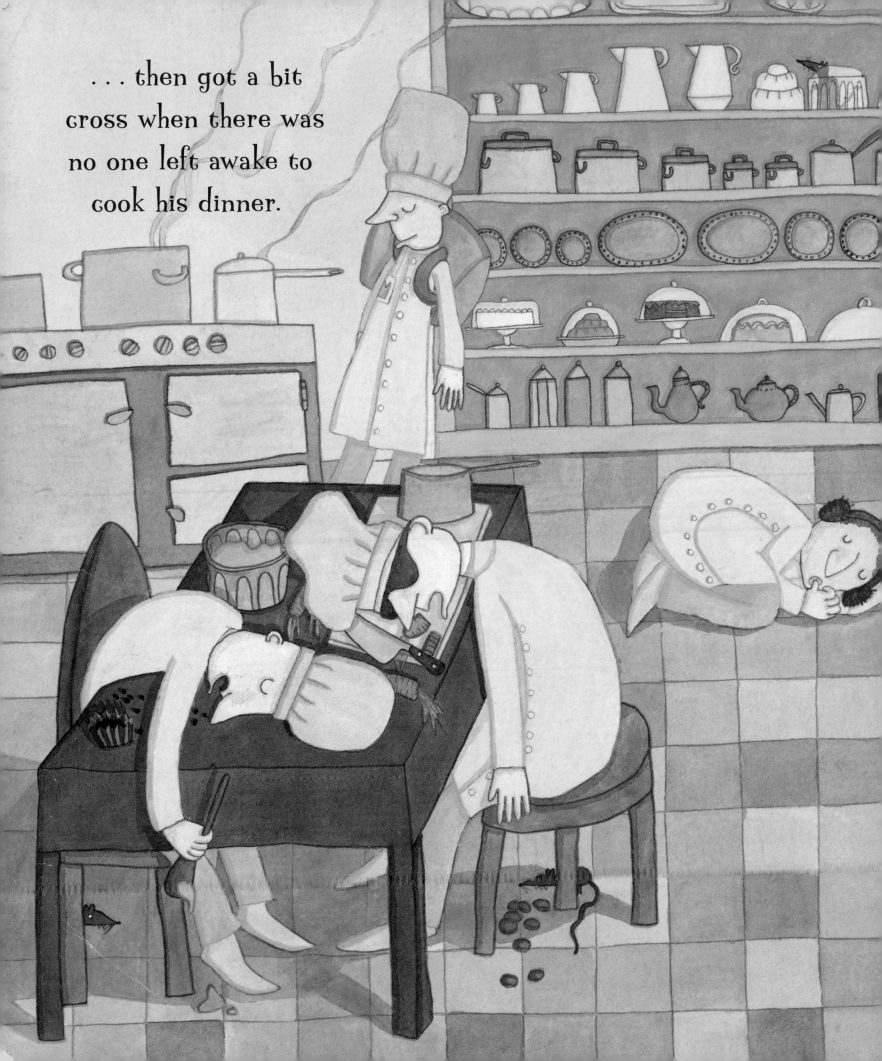

Many princes came

and many princes went,

but the king never slept.

Now all these comings and goings had been watched by a young farmer who worked in the fields outside the palace. One Monday morning, that very same farmer came to the palace and handed the king a basket.
"Ten fluffy chicks for the king," he announced.

The king opened the basket and said,
"That's not ten chicks! It's only **one**! Away with you!
My guards will show you out."

On Tuesday, the farmer returned carrying a wriggling bag.

"Ten long-eared rabbits for the king," he announced.

The king opened the bag and said, "That's not ten rabbits! It's only two, you foolish farmer! Go away!"

On Wednesday, the farmer returned carrying a large sack.
"Ten crowing cockerels for the king," he announced.

The king opened the sack and said, "That's not ten cockerels! It's only **three!**"

And he shooed the farmer out of the palace.

On Thursday, the farmer returned
carrying a heavy box.
"Ten playful puppies for the king,"
he announced.

The king opened the box and said,
"That's not ten puppies!
It's only **four**!
Stop wasting my time!"

On Friday, the farmer returned pulling a wooden cart. "Ten curly-tailed pigs for the king," he announced.

The king looked in the cart and said, "That's not ten pigs! It's only five! Get out!"

On Saturday, the farmer returned with a whole flock of sheep who bleated and baaed and jostled the guards outside the door.

"One hundred sheep for the king," he announced.

The king looked at the farmer and said, "You can't even count to ten. You'll never count to one hundred. I will count the animals myself."

"One, two, three . . ." the king counted carefully.

". . . fifteen, sixteen, seventeen . . .

. . . thirty-eight, thirty-nine, forty . . ."
The king stifled a yawn.

"... sixty-four, sixty-five, sixty-six ..."
The king's head began to droop.

"... ninety-one ... ninety-two ...
ninety-thrrrr ..."

ZZZZ z z

To the amazement of everyone (except
the farmer) the king was fast asleep!

So the king never did find the perfect prince, but he didn't mind because the princess was perfectly happy with the clever farmer. They had a huge wedding with singing and dancing and loads of delicious sandwiches and cakes.

And they all slept peacefully ever after.

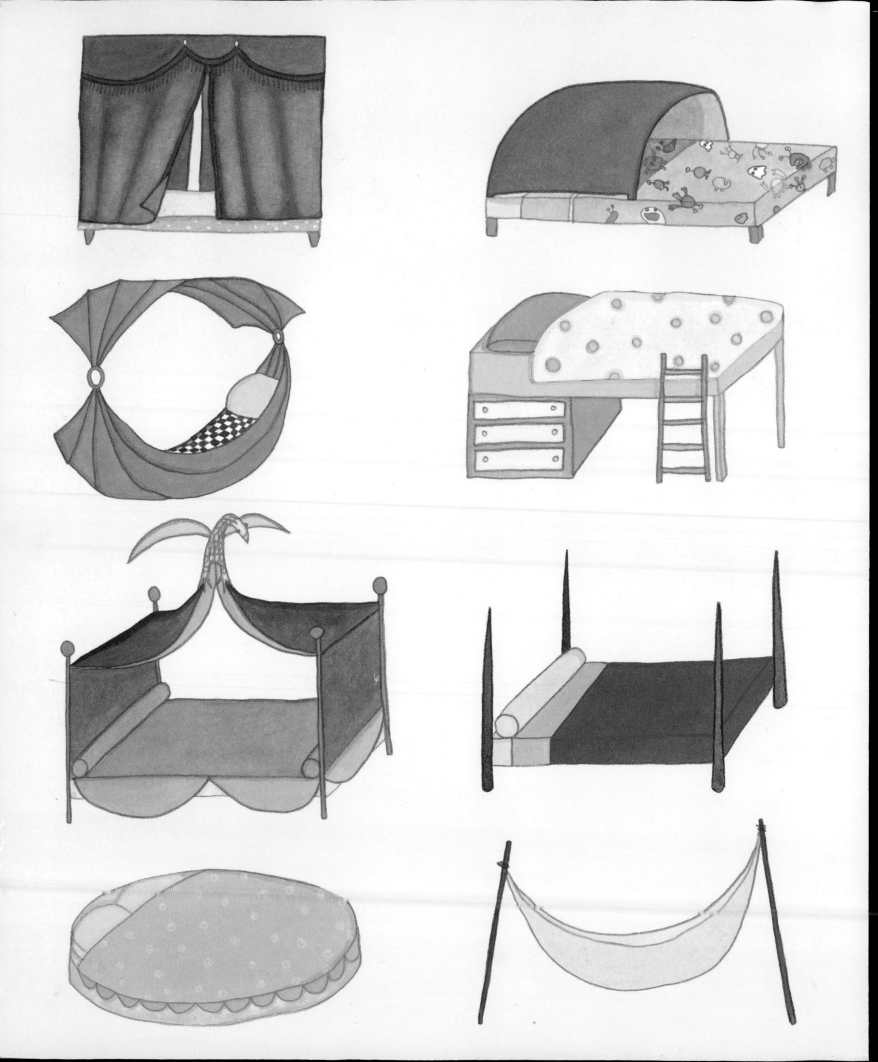

More books to enjoy:

9781849392082

9781849393126

9781849393874

9781849393843

9781849392259